SpongeBob SquarePants

Good Times!

by Erica David
based on the teleplay "The Great Escape" by Paul Tibbitt,
Steven Banks, Luke Brookshier, and Nate Cash
illustrated by The Artifact Group

Ready-to-Read

Simon Spotlight/Nickelodeon
New York   London   Toronto   Sydney

Stephen Hillenburg

Based on the TV series *SpongeBob SquarePants*® created by Stephen Hillenburg
as seen on Nickelodeon®

SIMON SPOTLIGHT
An imprint of Simon & Schuster Children's Publishing Division
1230 Avenue of the Americas, New York, New York 10020
© 2009 Viacom International Inc. All rights reserved. NICKELODEON, *SpongeBob SquarePants*, and all related titles, logos, and characters
are registered trademarks of Viacom International Inc.
For information about special discounts for bulk purchases, please contact
Simon & Schuster Sales at 1-866-506-1949 or business@simonandschuster.com
Manufactured in the United States of America

4 6 8 10 9 7 5 3
Library of Congress Cataloging-in-Publication Data
David, Erica.
Good times! / by Erica David ; illustrated by the Artifact Group. — 1st ed.
p. cm. — (Ready-to-read)
"Based on the TV series SpongeBob SquarePants created by Stephen Hillenburg as seen on Nickelodeon"—T.p. verso.
ISBN 978-1-4169-8500-6
1009 LAK
I. Artifact Group. II. SpongeBob SquarePants (Television program) III. Title.
PZ7.D28197Goo 2009
[E]—dc22
2009012398

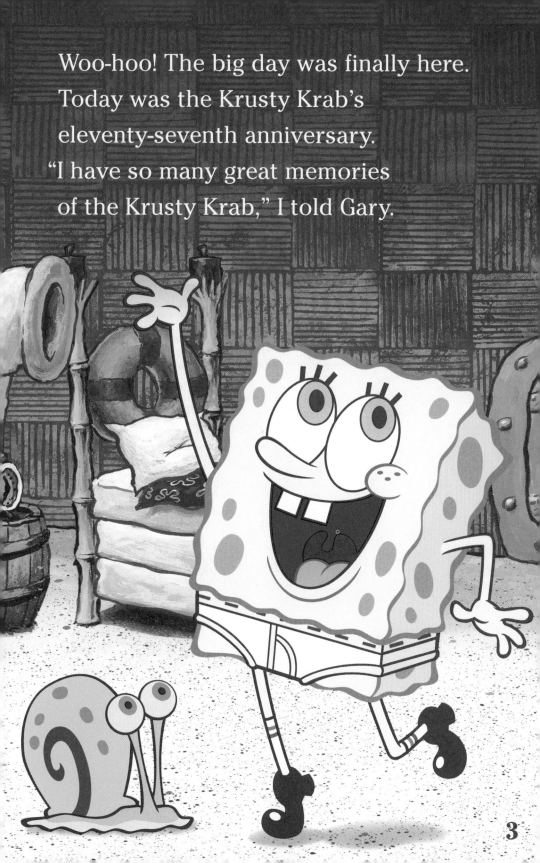

Woo-hoo! The big day was finally here. Today was the Krusty Krab's eleventy-seventh anniversary. "I have so many great memories of the Krusty Krab," I told Gary.

Love at First Bite

I remember my first Krabby Patty.
This was before I was even born!
Mom and Dad were looking for
a place to eat.

"How about this place?" Dad asked
as we stopped in front of the
Krusty Krab.
"What do you think, baby?"
Mom said. She did not
have to ask me twice!

"What would you like to eat?"
Mom asked. I looked out
through her belly button
at the menu board.
"Kwabbie Pabbie," I said.

It was the most amazing thing
I had ever tasted!
It was love at first bite.

On my way to work I spotted
an old Krabby Patty wrapper.
It reminded me of the first time
I saw the Krusty Krab on TV.

A Sack Full of Krabbies

I was sitting in front of the TV. Suddenly Krabby Patties popped onto the screen. They swirled around to a catchy song.

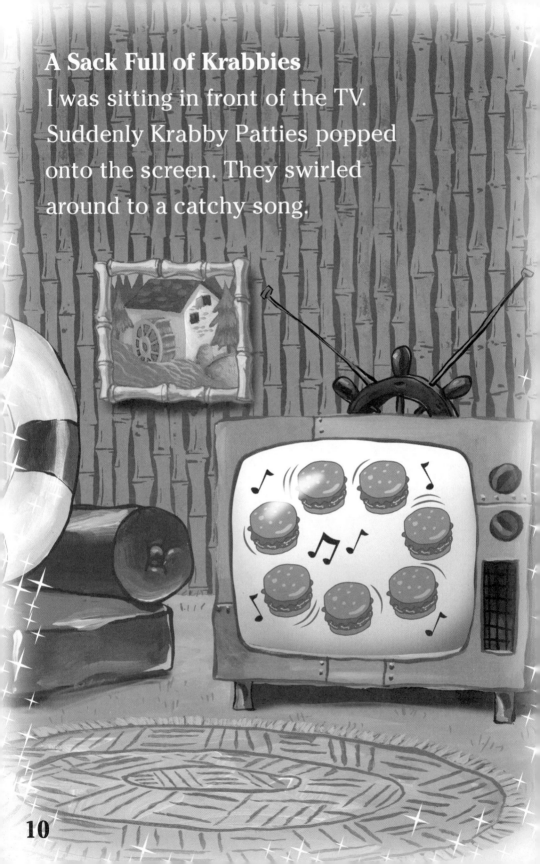

"Buy, buy, buy!" the song said. Then Mr. Krabs appeared, dressed like a doctor. "Go out and get a sack full of Krabbies!" he said. "They are good for your health."

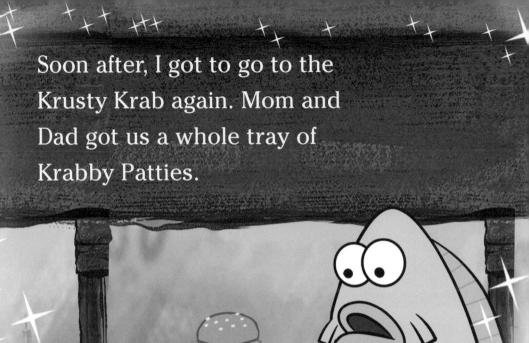

Soon after, I got to go to the
Krusty Krab again. Mom and
Dad got us a whole tray of
Krabby Patties.

I took one bite and my stomach
jumped for joy.
Mr. Krabs was right.
Krabby Patties **are** good for you!

At the Krusty Krab, Mr. Krabs
was very excited. He was
expecting a lot of people to show up
at the restaurant.

"Today's a big day," said Mr. Krabs.
"I want everyone to look out
   for Plankton."
He had a feeling Plankton would try to
steal the secret Krabby Patty recipe
on this special day.
"Aye, aye, sir!" I replied.

"It's up to us to keep the Krabby Patty recipe safe," I said. "That reminds me of the day you told me the secret recipe, Mr. Krabs."

A Dream Come True

"One day Mr. Krabs called me
into his office. He was going to
share the Krabby Patty recipe.
But first we had to go where
no one would hear us."

"First Mr. Krabs led me outside. We crossed a busy street. We walked and walked. Soon we reached the edge of Bikini Bottom. Still we kept walking. We hiked through a jungle.

Then we marched
across a desert."

"Next we crossed an old rope bridge.
We walked until my feet hurt.
I was getting tired. But finally
we came back to the Krusty Krab."

"What?" Squidward said. "You and
    Mr. Krabs just walked in a big circle?
    That is crazy!"
"No, it was the best day of my life,"
    I said. "I learned the secret recipe.
    It was a fry cook's dream come true."

"Well, **my** dream come true was
the day before you moved to
Bikini Bottom," Squidward said.
"Ha, ha, ha," I replied. "I know you
are glad I moved here."

Love Your Neighbor

"I'll never forget the day I moved
to Bikini Bottom," I said. "I looked
at a lot of houses, but none of them
felt like home. I was very sad."

FOR
SALE

"Then the most incredible thing happened. A pineapple fell from the sky! It landed right next to Squidward's house."

"Then I met Patrick. You two were my new neighbors! And now I am glad to say that you are my friends."

The Wedding

"Hey, remember when I married Sandy?"
I asked my friends. I recalled that day
so clearly. Sandy walked toward me
wearing a beautiful white dress.
She looked so pretty!

"SpongeBob, do you take Sandy as your
   wife?" the wedding official asked.

"I do," I replied.

"Sandy, do you take SpongeBob as your
   husband?" he asked Sandy.

"Sure 'nuf!" she said.

"I now pronounce you sponge and
squirrel," the wedding official said.
I leaned in to give Sandy a big kiss—
and bonked my nose on her helmet!

It turned out the wedding was just part of a play, but that was the best role I ever had. Well, besides the role of fry cook at the Krusty Krab!

Later Mr. Krabs opened the doors to
a restaurant full of happy customers.
"Ah, the Krusty Krab. It's the home
of good food, good friends, and good
times," I told Patrick.

"Happy eleventy-seventh anniversary, Krusty Krab!"